For Gabriella, the definitive
dance floor diva! ~ S S

For Sunny ~ R S

LITTLE TIGER
An imprint of Little Tiger Press Limited
1 Coda Studios, 189 Munster Road, London SW6 6AW
Imported into the EEA by Penguin Random House Ireland,
Morrison Chambers, 32 Nassau Street, Dublin D02 YH68
www.littletiger.co.uk

First published in Great Britain 2023

DOGGY DANCE OFF

STEVE SMALLMAN   ROBERT STARLING

DANCE FLOOR

LITTLE TIGER

LONDON

This is the place where the **cool dogs** meet,
They wag their tails and they stomp their feet,

Dancing to the rhythm of the disco beat!
Down at the big Doggy Dance Off.

The **music's** great, but who let Patch in?
Superstar DJ and very good at scratchin'!

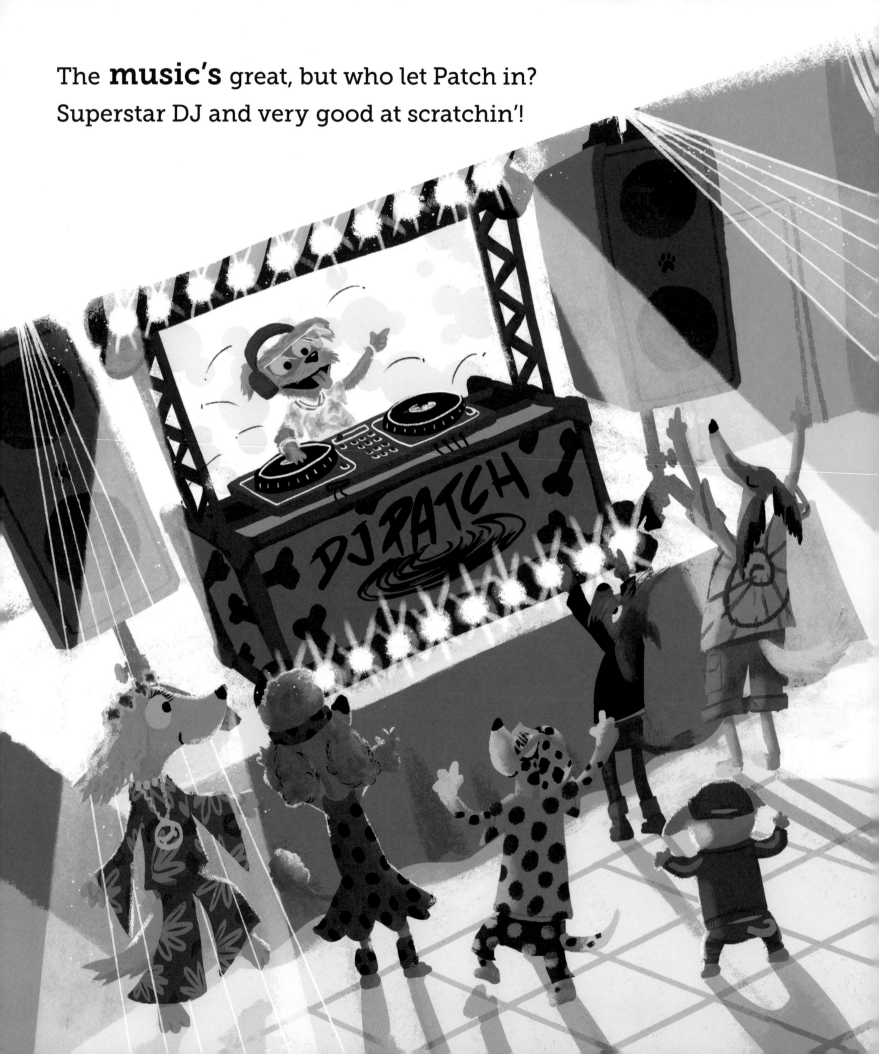

But he's got fleas,

and fleas

are catching!

Down at the
big Doggy Dance Off.

The crowd cheer Eva, the golden retriever,

Strutting up and down like a **dance floor diva!**

This party pooch has disco fever!
Down at the big Doggy Dance Off.

Better keep clear of **Dynamite Doug** . . .
A **cool** doggy dude and a body popping pug,

Spinning on his back like an upturned bug!
Down at the big Doggy Dance Off.

Onto the floor leapt
Duke Doggy Doo,

A pogoing, pink,
punk rocker cockapoo!

Bouncing all around like a mini kangaroo!

Woof

Down at the big Doggy Dance Off.

Caught in the spotlight, Lenny Labrador . . .
Who'd **never,** ever been to a disco before,

Got a bit **excited** and piddled on the floor!
Down at the big Doggy Dance Off.

The crowd stepped back
and called for a mop,

But a small, **masked** dancer
didn't want to stop!

She did a boogie woogie
to a spot of bebop!
Down at the big
Doggy Dance Off.

She did the funky chicken
and the hand jive too . . .

She did a **backflip**
and the crowd went . . .

WOOOO

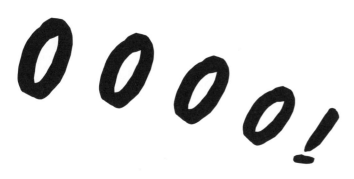

OOOO!

There wasn't any dance
this doggy couldn't do!
Down at the big Doggy Dance Off.

Who was the **stranger?**
Nobody could tell!
But they'd never, ever
seen a dog dance so well.

Then she **skidded** on the little
piddle puddle and she fell . . .

Down at the big Doggy Dance Off.

Her **mask** flew off

and so did her **hat**,

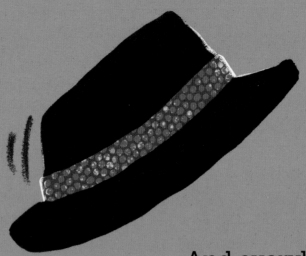

And everybody woofed,
"Well, fancy that!

This groovy mover's not a doggy, she's a . . . "

". . . CAT!"

A cat! At the big Doggy Dance Off?!

The cat looked scared then . . .

Duke Doggy Doo, Eva, Doug and little Lenny too,
Said, "Please can you show us how to dance like you?
You're the **Queen** of the **big Doggy Dance Off!**"

"Sure!" laughed the cat, **"Everybody follow me!"**
And she taught them her moves with a one, two, three!

Now cats and dogs dance together happily . . .
At **The All New Cat and Doggy Dance Off!**